Panda Cub House Family

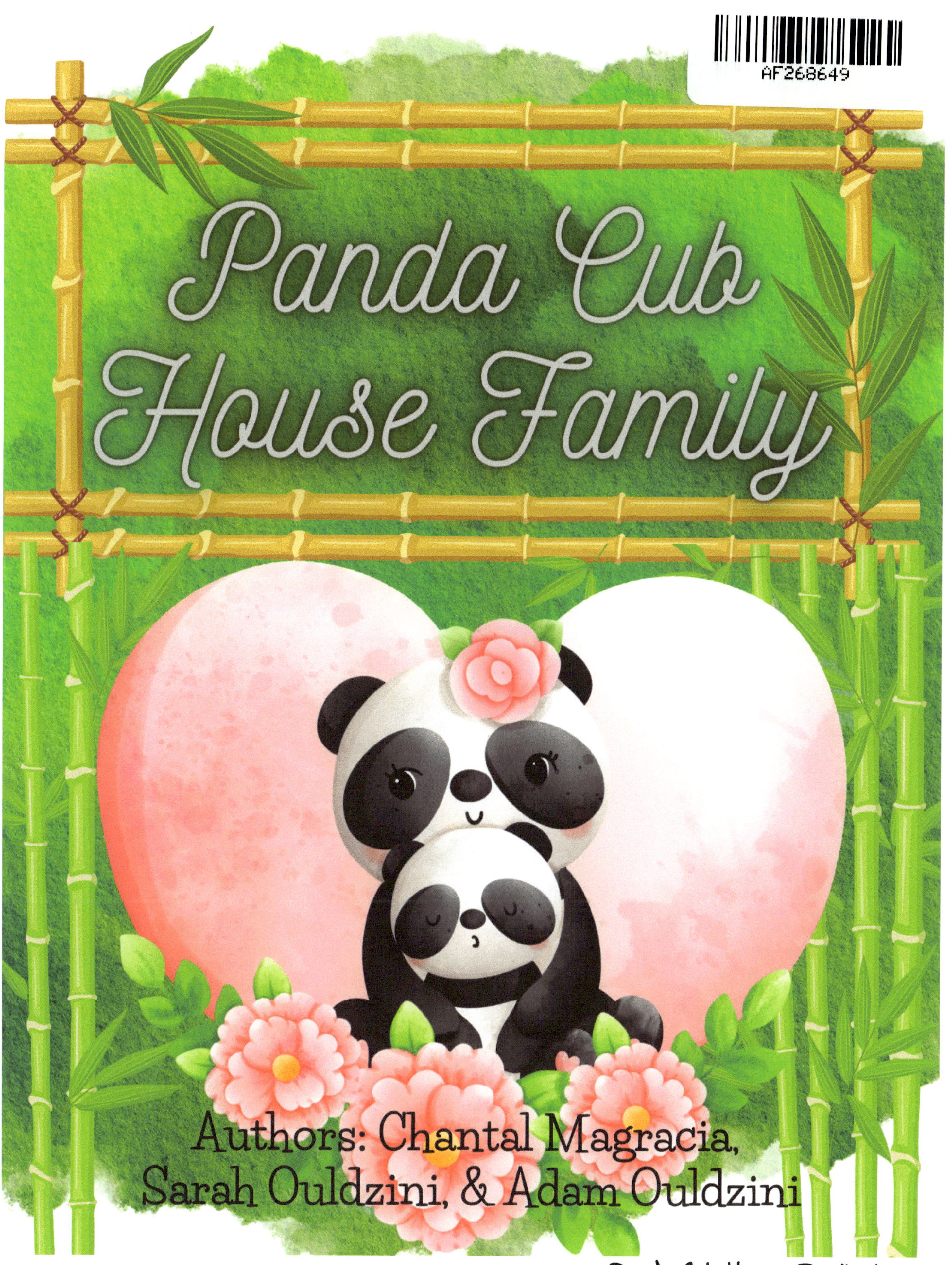

Authors: Chantal Magracia,
Sarah Ouldzini, & Adam Ouldzini

Panda Cub House Family 1

Panda Cub House Family

Authors:
Chantal V. Magracia - Ouldzini
Adam Ouldzini
Sarah Ouldzini

First published in Canada in 2023
by Chantal Magracia of PhilMorCan Press.
Copyright © 2022 Chantal Magracia
ISBN: 978-1-7772044-5-7

This book is a gift for:

This book is a gift from:

Panda Cub House Family 3

Panda Cub House
Family Protection &
Research Centre
Panda Cub House Family 4

My name is Toto.
I'm the cutest cub here.

I love cuddles and snuggles.
I love spending time with my family.
Would you like to meet my entire tribe?
Here, let me introduce you!

Panda Cub House Family 5

"My name is Mimi.
I'm Toto's older
sister.

We love to eat,
play, and sleep.

As for me,
I love to dance too.

Our Panda
Caretaker,
Ms. Miguela,
teaches us Zumba
so she's inspired
me to become a
ballerina.

I've got all the
moves.

Here, let me show
you my
performance for
the song, 'Pyotr
Ilyich Tchaikovsky's
Swan Lake'."

Panda Cub House Family 6

Swan Lake
Performance
Panda Cub House Family 7

Toto's the youngest panda cub in the house! Toto has the best older sister any panda could ever wish for – his older sister Mimi. Mimi likes to play with Toto and that makes Toto very happy.
They make time for each other to be together.
They have the most fun together.
They always find things to do together.
They never feel bored with each other.
Even during quiet times, they choose to stay together.
They're always there for one another.

Because Mamang always reminds Mimi,
"You only have one brother.
You have to love him and
you have to take care of him
because there's only two of you."

"Of course, Mamang! I love Toto so much.
I'll take care of him. No worries!"

Panda Cub House Family 9

This is our Papang.

He loves us.

He cares for us.

He built us our house.

He built us our playground.

He built us our eating corner.

He always does his best to provide for us.

Our Papang gathers bamboos for us so we never go hungry. He's extremely hard working.

Papang's Bamboo Delivery Service

Panda Cub House Family 11

Now you know exactly how hard
our Papang works.

He's here.
He's there.
He's everywhere.

When it comes to feeding time,
our Panda Caretaker, Ms.
Babina,
helps us eat together as a whole
family with our entire tribe.

She puts together all of the
bamboos.

Then, she places them nicely in
our eating corner.

Once she puts on
some calming music,
it's our signal to start eating.

Panda Cub House Family 12

After we eat, our Panda CareTaker,
Ms. Enaam puts us to bed because it's time for us to take a nap.

We nap not only once or twice but thrice.
We love resting, relaxing, chilling, and taking naps for sure!

She says we need to sleep to help us with our growth and development.
That may be true because we feel so re-energized whenever we take naps.
We feel so refreshed after.

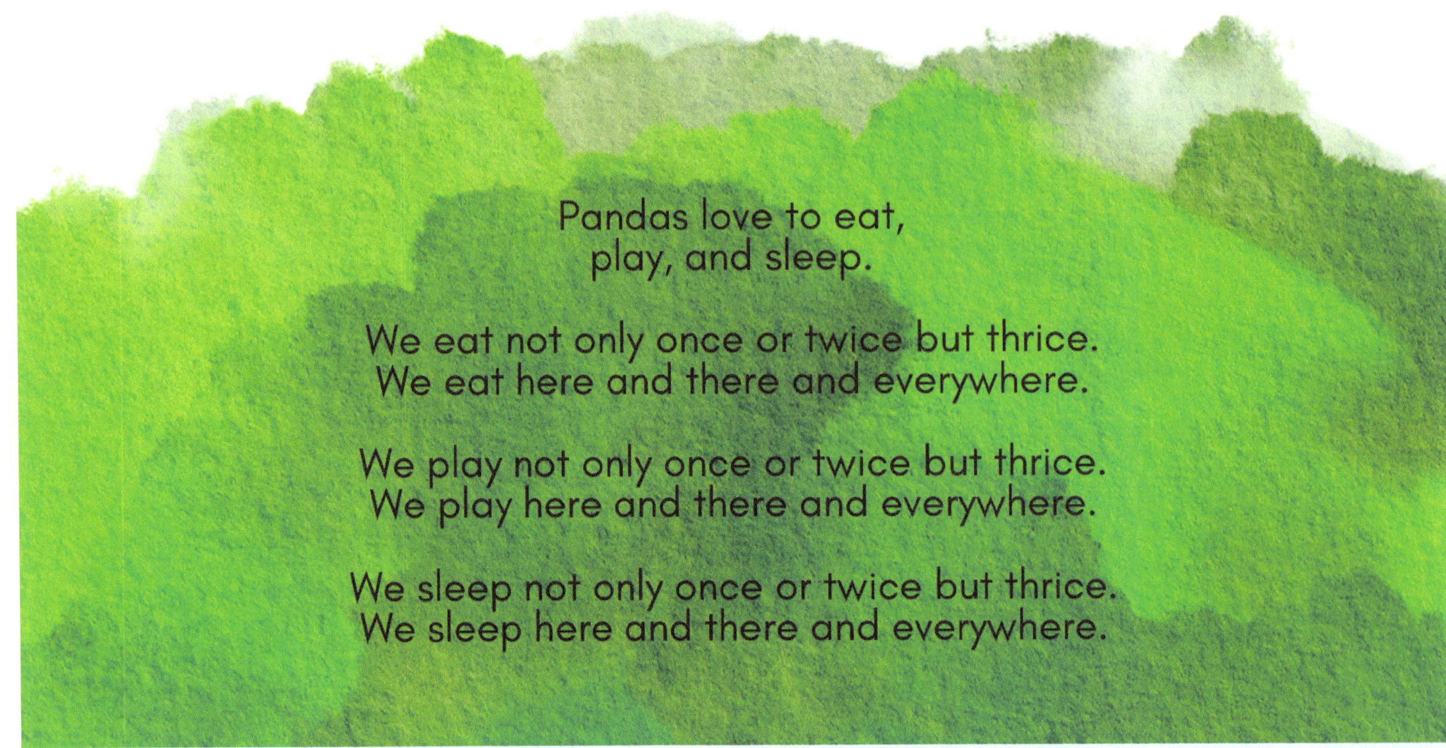

Pandas love to eat,
play, and sleep.

We eat not only once or twice but thrice.
We eat here and there and everywhere.

We play not only once or twice but thrice.
We play here and there and everywhere.

We sleep not only once or twice but thrice.
We sleep here and there and everywhere.

After our nap time, it's time for our Panda CareTaker, Ms. Jexy, to play with us!

It's honestly the most fun thing we do everyday.

We love to rumble and tumble down the hills.

We rumble and tumble once.

We rumble and tumble twice.

We rumble and tumble thrice.

Then we rest once we feel tired.

Panda Cub House Family 15

We love to play and play some more. So,

We love to roll and stroll down the mountainside.

We roll and stroll once.

We roll and stroll twice.

We roll and stroll thrice.

Then, we rest once we feel tired.

Panda Cub House
Family Protection
and
Research Centre

Mimi and Toto and all of us panda cubs usually play all day long.

Their Mamang and Papang always say that it's healthy for all of us to move around all the time since playing a lot makes us sweat and sweating is healthy!

Mamang usually says, "The more you play, the longer you'll live!"

Of course, for Mimi and Toto and the rest of us panda cubs – that is great news because we love to play!

By the end of the day, we feel so exhausted from playing.
We usually play non-stop for 5 hours straight!
Now, it's time for some quiet.
Our Panda CareTakers,
Ms. Jaspreet and Ms. Priyanka
usually takes the time to read to us their favourite books.

We can't read yet but we like to look at the pictures.

We love listening to stories because we learn a lot from them.

Some of the cubs
like to tear the books
and eat the pages
but they end up throwing up
after because the books taste gross.

We usually read not only one or two
but three books together!

We love it when it gets cold outside
because we've got more than enough fur for it.

Our Panda CareTaker, Ms. Rochelle bundles us up warmly and plays with us
outside in the snow. We make snow angels and igloos or we play hockey or ice
skating. No matter how cold it gets, we're always ready to have fun and play.
We play here and there and everywhere. We're always ready and prepared for
the weather!

Panda Cub House Family 19

"We have the best job in the world!
We are known as the Panda CareTakers.

We spend each day caring for 23 panda cubs
at the 'Panda Cub House Family Protection and
Research Centre'.

We prepare their meals of bamboo and milk
formula.

We check on their growth and health and
development.

We carry these two-tonne fluff balls between
their sleeping pens.

Most importantly, the best part of our job is
that we get to cuddle them and snuggle them
all the time."

Panda Cub House Family 20

"We feed them,
bathe them,
cuddle them,
snuggle them,
protect them,
nurse them,
love them,
care for them, and
play with them.

It's the best job indeed!"

Thank You, Panda Cub House Team!
LOVE
Thank You Ms. Miguela for always dancing with us. We love dancing Zumba with you. You deserve this cup of delicious hot chocolate!
Love,
Panda Cubs in the House
Panda Cub House Family 22

Thank You, Panda Cub House Team!

Thank You Ms. Babina for always feeding us. We love eating with you. You deserve this cup of delicious salted caramel cappucino!

Love,
Panda Cubs in the House
Panda Cub House Family 23

Thank You, Panda Cub House Team!
Thank You Ms. Enaam for always helping us rest and relax. We love relaxing with you. You deserve this cup of delicious hot chocolate!
Love,
Panda Cubs in the House
Panda Cub House Family 24

Thank You, Panda Cub House Team!
Thank You Ms. Jexy for always playing with us. We love playing with you. You deserve this cup of delicious strawberry milkshake!
Love,
Panda Cubs in the House
Panda Cub House Family 25

Thank You, Panda Cub House Team!
BE MINE
Thank You Ms. Jaspreet for always reading books for us. We love reading with you. You deserve this cup of delicious salted caramel cappucino!
Love,
Panda Cubs in the House
Panda Cub House Family 26

Thank You, Panda Cub House Team!
Thank You Ms. Priyanka for always having fun with us. We love spending time with you. You deserve this cup of delicious hot chocolate!
Love,
Panda Cubs in the House
Panda Cub House Family 27

Thank You, Panda Cub House Team!

Thank You Ms. Rochelle for always bringing us outdoors especially when it's cold out! We love spending time with you outdoors. You deserve this cup of delicious hot chocolate!

Love,
Panda Cubs in the House
Panda Cub House Family 28

Thank You, Panda Cub House Team!
Thank You to the owners of the Panda Cub House Family Protection & Research Centre, Jun & Ludy. We absolutely love it here. You deserve this cup of delicious salted caramel cappucino!
Love,
Panda Cubs in the House
Panda Cub House Family 29

Welcome to the
Panda Cub House
Colouring Pages

MOM

Panda Cub House Family 32

MOM
Panda Cub House Family 33

Panda Cub House Family 34

Panda Cub House Family 35

Panda Cub House Family 36

Panda Cub House Family 37

Panda Cub House Family 38

Panda Cub House Family 39

Panda Cub House Family 40

Panda Cub House Family 41

Panda Cub House Family 42

 Panda Cub House Teachers 🐼

In Real Life

pandacubhouse.com

Panda Cub House Family 43

About The Author

Chantal Magracia is a Filipino-Canadian author, educator, entrepreneur, and philanthropist, who graduated with a Bachelor of Education degree from the University of Alberta. She is currently pursuing higher education from the University of British Columbia.

She is an experienced teacher who has taught K-12 students, including adult learners since 2011 in Alberta, Canada. She is a permanently licensed educator both in Alberta, Canada and British Columbia, Canada.

She has always been extremely passionate about Character Education which encompasses values, principles, ethics, morals, virtues, good manners, right conduct, and proper etiquette. In her work, she is highly driven to model what empathy, compassion, kindness, acceptance, consideration, thoughtfulness, and understanding looks like in our daily lives. She's a dedicated and devoted life-long learner with great work ethics, who prefers to write children's books as her medium of choice, to share her learnings, reflections, epiphanies, wisdom, and growth regarding her constant pursuit of becoming the best version of herself simply by helping and uplifting others.

Hello PANDA Lovers,

Welcome to the Panda Cub House Family Protection & Research Centre. We will show you why we love it here so much and why we love being a PANDA! Being a PANDA is the best thing to be in the entire world! What do we do? We just have fun and enjoy life!

We also express our heartfelt gratitude to our Panda CareTakers for loving us and taking care of us. We're also extremely grateful to you for not allowing our species to go extinct! As a token of our appreciation, we've included some CUTE PANDA Colouring Pages for you and your loved ones to enjoy together! Have fun!